From the best-selling book *Tell Me the Story* written by Max Lucado, created by Ron DiCianni

# The Children of the King

# Max Lucado

## Illustrated by Toni Goffe

CROSSWAY BOOKS • WHEATON, ILLINOIS

A DIVISION OF GOOD NEWS PUBLISHERS

PUBLISHER'S ACKNOWLEDGEMENT

The publisher wishes to acknowledge that the text for *The Children of the King*
appeared originally in *Tell Me the Story*, written by Max Lucado and illustrated by
Ron DiCianni. Special thanks to Ron DiCianni for the idea and vision behind
the creation of *Tell Me the Story*. For more stories in the "Tell Me" series, *Tell Me
the Story* and *Tell Me the Secrets*, both published by Crossway Books, are
available at your local bookstore.

*The Children of the King*

Published by Crossway Books
      a division of Good News Publishers
      1300 Crescent Street
      Wheaton, Illinois 60187.

Cover illustration: Toni Goffe

Printed in Mexico

ISBN 0-89107-823-1

*To*
*Justin, Kendall, and Taylor*

ALONG TIME AGO in a land much like your own, there was a village. And in this village lived five orphans. A lonely family of fatherless children, they had banded together against the cold. One day a king learned of their misfortune and decided to adopt them. He decreed that he would be their father and planned to come for them.

All the people in the land thought it odd that the king should adopt these children. He already had many people to care for.

"Why does the king want them?" the people would ask. But the king had his reasons.

When the children learned that they had a new father, and their father was *the king* (no less!), and the king was coming to visit, they went wild with excitement.

When the people of the village learned that the children had a father, and their father was *the king*, and that the king was coming to the village, they were terribly excited as well. They went out to see the children and told them what to do.

"You need to impress the king," they explained. "Only those with great gifts to give will be allowed to live in the castle."

The people didn't know the king. They just assumed that all kings want to be impressed.

So the children worked long and hard preparing their offerings. One boy, who knew how to carve, determined to give the king a wonderful work of wooden art. He set his knife against the soft skin of the elm and whittled. The small blocks of wood came alive with the eyes of a sparrow or the nose of a unicorn.

His sister decided to present the king with a painting that captured the beauty of the heavens— a painting worthy to hang in his castle.

Another sister chose music as her way to impress the king. For long hours she practiced with her voice and mandolin. Village people would stop at her window and listen as her music took wings and soared.

Yet another child set out to turn the king's head with his wisdom. Late hours would find his candle lit and his books open. Geography. Mathematics. Chemistry. The breadth of his study was matched only by the depth of his desire. Surely a sage such as the king would appreciate all his hard work.

But there was one little girl who had nothing to offer. Her hand was clumsy with the knife, her fingers stiff with the brush. She opened her mouth to sing, but the sound was hoarse. She was too dull to read. She had no talent. She had no gift.

All she had to offer was her heart, for her heart was good. She spent her time at the city gates, watching the people come and go. She would make pennies by grooming their horses or feeding their animals. A stable girl she was—a stable girl with no stable. But she had a good heart.

She knew the beggars by name. She took time to pet each dog.
She welcomed home the travelers and greeted the strangers.

"How was the journey?" she would ask.

"Tell me what you learned on your visit."

"How is your husband?"

"Do you enjoy your new work?"

She was full of questions for people because her heart was big
and she cared about people.

But since she had no talent and no gift, she grew anxious that the king would be angry. The villagers told her that the king would want a gift and that she should set her mind about the task of making one. So she took a small knife and went to her brother, the carver.

"Could you teach me to carve?" she asked.

"Sorry," the young crafter responded without looking up. "I've much work to do. I haven't time for you. The king is coming, you know."

The girl put away her knife and picked up a brush. She went to her sister, the artist. She found her on a hill painting a sunset on a canvas.

"You paint so well," said the girl who had no gift but a big heart.

"I know," the painter answered.

"Could you share with me your gift?"

"Not now," the sister responded with eyes on her palette. "The king is coming, you know."

The girl with no gift then remembered her other sister, the one with the song. "She will help me," she said. But when she arrived at her sister's house, she found a crowd of people waiting to listen to her sister sing.

"Sister," she called, "sister, I've come to listen and learn." But her sister couldn't hear. The noise of the applause was too loud.

Heart heavy, the girl turned and walked away.

Then she remembered her other brother. She took a book with small words and big letters and went to see him. "I have nothing to offer the king," she said. "Could you teach me to read so I might show him my wisdom?"

The young sage-to-be didn't speak. He was lost in thought. The child with no gift spoke again. "Could you help me? I have no talent—"

"Go away," said the scholar, scarcely moving his eyes from the text. "Can't you see I'm preparing myself for the coming of the king?"

And so the girl went away sorrowfully. She had nothing to give.

She returned to her place at the city gates and took up her task of caring for people's animals.

   After some days a man in merchant's dress came to the small town.

   "Can you feed my donkey?" he asked the girl. The orphan jumped to her feet and looked into the brown face of the one who had traveled far. His skin was leathery from the sun, and his eyes were deep. A kind smile from beneath the beard warmed the girl.

"That I can," the girl answered and eagerly took the animal to the trough. "Trust him with me. When you return, he will be groomed and fed."

"Tell me," she asked as the donkey drank, "have you come to stay?"

"For only a while."

"Are you weary from your journey?"

"That I am."

"Would you like to sit and rest?" The girl motioned to a bench near the wall.

The tall man with the dark skin sat on the bench, leaned against the wall, closed his eyes, and slept.

After a few minutes he opened them and found
the girl sitting at his feet, looking at his face.
She was embarrassed that he had caught her
staring. She turned away.

"Have you sat there long?"

"Yes."

"What do you seek?"

"Nothing. You seem to be a kind man with a peaceful heart. It's good to be near you."

The man smiled and stroked his beard. "You are a wise girl," he said. "When I return, we will visit more."

The man did return—quite soon.
"Did you find whom you sought?" the girl asked.
"I found them, but they were too busy for me."
"What do you mean?"

"Those I came to see were too busy to see me. One was a woodsmith rushing to complete a project. He told me to return tomorrow. Another was an artist. I saw her sitting on a hillside, but the people below said she did not want to be disturbed. The other was a musician. I sat with the others and listened to her music. When I asked to talk with her, she said she had no time. The other I sought had left. He has moved to the city to go to school."

The girl's eyes widened.

"But you don't look like a king," she gasped.

"I try not to," he explained. "Being a king can be lonely. People act strangely around me. They ask for favors. They try to impress me. They bring me all their complaints."

"But isn't that what a king is for?" asked the girl.

"Certainly," responded the king, "but there are times when I just want to be with my people. There are times when I want to talk to my people—to hear about their day, to laugh a bit, to cry some. There are times when I just want to be their father."

"Is that why you adopted the children?"
"That's why. Children like to talk. Adults think they have to impress me; children don't. They just want to talk to me."
"But my brothers and sisters were too busy?"
"They were. But I'll come back. Maybe they'll have more time another day."

"Would you like to ride on my donkey to the castle?"
And so it happened that the children with many talents but no time missed the visit of the king, while the girl whose only gift was her time to talk became his child.